Written by Alei

The Virtue of

Prudence

LOYOLA PRESS.

Why is it necessary to teach prudence?

In a world that encourages quick decision-making and instant gratification, teaching the virtue of prudence is more important than ever. Prudence means taking the time needed to make a carefully considered decision, and then proceeding with caution in a measured way. It does not mean being frozen in place by cumbersome reflection. Instead, prudence gives us the confidence and freedom to act on the decisions we make. It's important that children are taught that a decision comes before every action, large and small, each day. Children can be guided to exercise the virtue of prudence in many ways that will help build their capacity for sound decision-making. Making lists and schedules can help children develop the habit of being prepared, which is an important component of prudence. Encourage children to consider not only the effect a decision will have on themselves but also the effect it will have on others. The ability to slow down and do what is right is a virtue that only becomes more important as children grow into teenagers and then adults.

Spaghetti is
so good!

4

I like spaghetti so much that
I gobble one forkful after another.
One, two, three, forgetting that
there is something else I also like a
lot. Dessert! If only I had thought
about that before. Now I'm too
full to enjoy it.

I got lost!

"Hold our hands," Mom and Dad always tell me. But
I got distracted today and got lost. "Where are they?"
I shout! I cry! Then I remember what Dad's hat looks

like and what color Mom's coat is. I look for a green hat and a red coat. I stay in place so they can find me. Here they come!

The wise Cow

8

I have a cow at home. It's a little clay bank with small ears and big eyes. It seems to look at me every time I have a coin and am thinking about spending it to buy candy. "Give it to me," it seems to say to me. "When my tummy is full, you'll be able to buy something you want more, something that will last longer."

Who did it?

I don't know how it happened, but some black paint got on Dad's papers—large black spots and smudges. Maybe the paint fell from the ceiling or blew in from the street. No, that's not believable. It was hard, but I told Dad what really happened. "I'm sorry. It was me," I said to Dad. He smiled and gave me a paintbrush. "Here, this time paint at your table, OK?"

Tag, you're it!

"Why do you always win when we play blindfold tag?" I ask a friend. "It's not a secret," he says. "You have to stay calm and not turn toward every sound you hear. Walk slowly, and don't forget to listen carefully. The sounds the others make will tell you where they are."

The disappearing notebook

"Somebody has taken my notebook. I think it was somebody from class," I told my teacher, seeing that my notebook was not in my backpack. She calmed me down by saying, "Wait before accusing anybody. Think about when you used it last, where you were, and what you were doing." I did what my teacher said. Then I opened my desk, and there it was! I had forgotten.

Raining oranges

When we go to the store, my brothers and I play a game to see who can put the food we need in the cart first. "Five oranges," says Dad. Then we all run off to find them. One time, I was in such a hurry that I forgot to take the oranges from the top of the display. I took one from the bottom, and they all fell on my head. "Hey, it's raining oranges!" exclaimed the grocer.

The shy cat

My aunt has a cat you can't pick up.
I always chase him around until he hides
under the couch. "Leave him be," the
adults tell me. "The more you try to
catch him, the more scared he will be."

This time, I don't do anything. I wait until he comes to me. And yes, he gets more trusting and comes right up to me.

Hat's off

"What do you think of my hat?" asks my mother proudly. It looks like she's wearing a chicken on her head, but I can't tell her that. So I look for the right words to tell her the truth in a kind way that won't hurt her feelings. "It hides your hair too much, and your hair is very nice. Maybe you can find a better hat." Pleased with what I had said, we both left the store with new hats.

The new Kid

At the start of each school year, there always seems to be a new child in class. This time it's me! My new classmates seem like they aren't quite sure what to think of me at first. I know they're wondering whether I would make a good friend. I'll do just what Mom and Dad told me. I'll introduce myself and be kind to everyone. Then I will make friends in no time.

Different bins for different things

After dinner, it's time to clean up the kitchen. Sometimes I throw all the trash into the same bin because I'm always in a hurry to go out to play. At home, we have different colored bins for separating the plastic and paper from the rest of the garbage. It takes a bit longer to put the things in the right bins, but that way we help the planet.

25

Red, the color that warns us

Just like a red traffic light tells cars when to stop, the red flag on the beach tells us that we're not allowed to swim. "We might get hurt," Mom explains when she sees our sad faces. Then she takes out a shovel and rake and exclaims, "But nobody says we can't make a sandcastle!"

Berry Careful

We get home with a basket full of berries that we gathered while we were outside. We shout, "Grandma, let's bake our berries in a pie!" She looks at the berries and says, "Not so fast. First, we need to look at them very carefully. Nature talks to us and tells us which ones are good and which ones are not. Look, those bright blue ones will give us all tummy aches. But the raspberries and blackberries will make a delicious pie!"

Fun in the sun

I love swim lessons, especially on sunny days. I wear my bathing suit and bring a towel. I wiggle and squirm as Mom and Dad help me put on sunscreen. "I don't want to put on sunscreen. I want to leave for my swim lessons now," I say. When I get to the pool, my swim teacher thanks me for coming prepared for the lesson with my sunscreen on and all ready to go.

A lake of birds

The last time we were here, it was too noisy and all the birds had been frightened away. Now I know that I have to be quiet and wait a while to see the ducks come out of their hiding places or for a seagull to dive into the water to catch a frog. "With the binoculars, you'll see better," whispers my uncle.

Parents' guide

TEACHING THE VIRTUE OF PRUDENCE

Children who practice the virtue of prudence often share the following characteristics:

- Admit mistakes.
- Take care of their possessions and respect the possessions of others.
- Have access to and seek the advice of caring adults.
- Avoid being rushed into decisions.
- Demonstrate an awareness of the consequences of an action or decision.
- Are aware of the value of money.
- Plan ahead.

PRUDENCE AND RESPECT FOR OTHERS

Empathy is an important building block of the virtue of prudence. Guiding children to see how their words and actions affect others helps them become more prudent. When choosing between two good things, encourage your child to choose the one that wouldn't hurt others and is the kind choice.

PRUDENCE AND RESPECT FOR NATURAL RESOURCES

Exercising the virtue of prudence means not being wasteful. Be cognizant of how your family cares for the resources you use. Take the time to recycle materials appropriately and use electricity and water responsibly.

PRUDENCE WITH MONEY

Help children develop the habits necessary to make informed buying decisions rather than succumb to impulse purchases. You can model this by making a grocery list before going shopping and invite your child to help you compare prices. You may also want to make saving for an item or an outing to enjoy as a family something to work on together. Setting goals and achieving them through hard work and sacrifice help children exercise the skills necessary to make their own decisions in a prudent manner.

TIPS FOR PARENTS

- Provide discipline that is fair and consistent.
- Encourage and model reflection and careful consideration.
- Model prudent decision-making.
- Consider as a family the meaning and implication of adages, such as "A stitch in time saves nine," "Look before you leap," "An ounce of prevention is worth a pound of cure," and "Better safe than sorry."
- Discuss the actions of characters in books, movies, and in TV series.
- Admit your own mistakes, misjudgments, and miscalculations. Share how you would do things differently knowing what you know now. Help your child engage in this kind of after-action evaluation.
- Exercise prudence in electronic communication, including social media posts, emails, and texts.
- Invite your child to be part of planning for a family vacation, celebration, or trip to the grocery store.
- Help children review their own decision-making process as well as the consequences of their actions, both positive and negative.
- Play games, such as tic-tac-toe, checkers, and chess to help children think ahead.
- Rehearse situations that may require decision-making, such as choosing a book from the library or a gift for a friend, and how best to approach it.
- Avoid saying "I told you so."
- Never forget that a virtue is taught by experiencing it.

CLASSROOM RESOURCES

Visit **www.LoyolaPress.com/Virtues** to access activities centered on social–emotional learning that supplement the messages from *The Virtue of Prudence*.

LOYOLA PRESS.

3441 N. Ashland Avenue
Chicago, Illinois 60657
(800) 621-1008
www.loyolapress.com

THE VIRTUE OF PRUDENCE

Text: **Aleix Cabrera and Vinyet Montaner**

Illustration: **Rosa M. Curto**

Design and layout: **Estudi Guasch, S.L.**

© Gemser Publications, S.L. 2013

El Castell, 38   08329 Teià (Barcelona, Spain)

www.mercedesros.com

Published in the United States in 2020 by Loyola Press.
ISBN: 978-0-8294-5035-4
Library of Congress Control Number: 2020930994
Printed in China.